TITCHY WITCH
and the
Magic
Party

For Beccy
R.I.

To Nichy-noo
K.M.

Orchard Books
96 Leonard Street, London EC2A 4XD
Orchard Books Australia
32/45-51 Huntley Street, Alexandria, NSW 2015
First published in Great Britain in 2003
First paperback publication 2004
ISBN 1 84121 054 4 (HB)
ISBN 1 84121 130 3 (PB)
Text © Rose Impey 2003 Illustrations © Katharine McEwen 2003
The rights of Rose Impey to be identified as the author and
Katharine McEwen to be identified as the illustrator of this Work
have been asserted by them in accordance with the
Copyright, Designs and Patents Act, 1988.
A CIP catalogue record for this book is available from the British Library
1 3 5 7 9 10 8 6 4 2 (HB)
1 3 5 7 9 10 8 6 4 2 (PB)
Printed in Hong Kong

TITCHY WITCH

and the

Magic Party

Rose Impey ★ Katharine McEwen

ORCHARD BOOKS

Titchy-witch

Victor

Eric

Wendel

Weeny-witch

Witchy-witch

Cat-a-bogus

It was almost Halloween.
Witchy-witch and Wendel were
having a big party.

Titchy-witch wanted a party too.
"Of course, my little bewitcher,"
said Mum. "Cat-a-bogus will
do the food."

Oh, really?

Titchy-witch wanted all
her favourite things.

Mounds of maggot and
marmalade sandwiches,
piles of slug and pickle pizzas,
mountains of frogspawn jelly
and a colossal cake.

Yum! Yum!

Titchy-witch made a list of party
games too.

1. Musical
   broomsticks.

2. Pass the
   cauldron.

3. Crab-apple
   bobbing.

4.

And prizes!
"Big bags of Wiggly Wagglies and
Drobble-drops and Squibblies."

"I hope no-one's sick," said
Cat-a-bogus.

But then Titchy-witch didn't know
who to invite to her party.

Primrose was really prissy.

And Gobby-goblin poked her all
the time.

And Wilfy-wolf played
tricks on her.

And Clever Jack was the
teacher's pet.

"Haven't got any friends," said
Titchy-witch.
"Well, a party's a good way to
make some," said Wendel.

But when the party arrived,
Titchy-witch didn't think
she was going to enjoy
it very much.

She scowled when Clever
Jack won all the Drobble-drops.

She gritted her fangs when
Gobby-goblin cheated at
Crab-Apple Bobbing.

And when Primrose won at
Musical Broomsticks, she was so
cross she wiggled her nose...

...and made Primrose's broomstick disappear.

Mum and Dad told her to hand
round the food and be
a good little witch.
But she wasn't.

Suddenly Primrose
had a tail.

Clever Jack grew a pair of
rabbit's ears.

Gobby-goblin started
breathing fire.

And Wilfy-Wolf found he could fly.

Mum and Dad nearly put a stop to it.

But everyone was having such a good time.

"You are clever," said Clever Jack.
"I wish I was a witch, like you,"
said Primrose.

Even Gobby-goblin asked Titchy-witch to come to his cave for tea.

At the end of the party Cat-a-bogus was waiting at the door. He made sure everyone went home the same as they had come.

Well, almost every one.

"Please let me keep it," begged
Primrose. "Just till Monday."
"All right," said Titchy-witch.

Primrose gave her a big hug.
"You're my best friend ever,"
she said.

TITCHY WITCH

Rose Impey ★ Katharine McEwen

Enjoy a little more magic with all the Titchy-witch tales:

- ❏ Titchy-witch and the Birthday Broomstick   1 84121 044 7
- ❏ Titchy-witch and the Disappearing Baby   1 84121 040 4
- ❏ Titchy-witch and the Frog Fiasco   1 84121 046 3
- ❏ Titchy-witch and the Stray Dragon   1 84121 042 0
- ❏ Titchy-witch and the Bully-Boggarts   1 84121 048 X
- ❏ Titchy-witch and the Wobbly Fang   1 84121 050 1
- ❏ Titchy-witch and the Get-Better Spell   1 84121 052 8
- ❏ Titchy-witch and the Magic Party   1 84121 054 4

All priced at £8.99 each

Colour Crunchies are available from all good
bookshops, or can be ordered direct from the publisher:
Orchard Books, PO BOX 29, Douglas IM99 1BQ
Credit card orders please telephone 01624 836000
or fax 01624 837033
or e-mail: bookshop@enterprise.net for details.

To order please quote title, author and ISBN
and your full name and address.
Cheques and postal orders should be
made payable to 'Bookpost plc'.
Postage and packing is FREE within the UK
(overseas customers should add £1.00 per book).

Prices and availability are subject to change.